How My Parents Learned to Eat

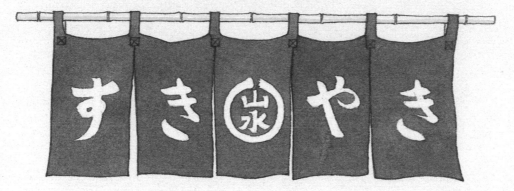

Ina R. Friedman

Illustrated by Allen Say

HOUGHTON MIFFLIN COMPANY BOSTON

Library of Congress Cataloging in Publication Data

Friedman, Ina R.
  How my parents learned to eat.

  Summary: An American sailor courts a Japanese girl
and each tries, in secret, to learn the other's way of eating.
  [1. Japan—Fiction. 2. Tableware—Fiction.
3. Manners and customs—Fiction] I. Say, Allen, ill.
II. Title.
PZ7.F8975Ho 1984   [E]   83-18553
ISBN 0-395-35379-3

Text copyright © 1984 by Ina Friedman
Illustrations copyright © 1984 by Allen Say

All rights reserved. No part of this work may be
reproduced or transmitted in any form or by any means,
electronic or mechanical, including photocopying and
recording, or by any information storage or retrieval
system, except as may be expressly permitted by the 1976
Copyright Act or in writing from the publisher. Requests
for permission should be addressed in writing to Houghton
Mifflin Company, 2 Park Street, Boston, Massachusetts 02108.

Printed in the United States of America

RNF   ISBN 0-395-35379-3
PAP   ISBN 0-395-44235-4

RNF P & PAP N 10 9 8 7

In our house, some days we eat with chopsticks
and some days we eat with knives and forks.
For me, it's natural.

When my mother met my father, she was a Japanese schoolgirl and he was an American sailor. His ship was stationed in Yokohama.

Every day, my father, whose name is John, walked in the park with my mother, Aiko. They sat on a bench and talked. But my father was afraid to invite my mother to dinner.

If we go to a restaurant, he thought, I'll go hungry because I don't know how to eat with chopsticks. And if I go hungry, I'll act like a bear. Then Aiko won't like me. I'd better not ask her to dinner.

My mother wondered why my father never invited her to dinner. Perhaps John is afraid I don't know how to eat with a knife and fork and I'll look silly, she thought. Maybe it is best if he doesn't invite me to dinner.

So they walked and talked and never ate a bowl of rice or a piece of bread together.

One day, the captain of my father's ship said,
"John, in three weeks the ship is leaving Japan."

My father was sad. He wanted to marry my mother.
How can I ask her to marry me? he thought. I don't
even know if we like the same food. And if we don't,
we'll go hungry. It's hard to be happy if you're hungry.
I'll have to find out what food she likes. And I'll have
to learn to eat with chopsticks.

So he went to a Japanese restaurant.

Everyone sat on cushions around low tables. My father bowed to the waiter. "Please, teach me to eat with chopsticks."

"Of course," said the waiter, bowing.

The waiter brought a bowl of rice and a plate of sukiyaki. Sukiyaki is made of small pieces of meat, vegetables, and tofu. It smelled good. My father wanted to gobble it up.

The waiter placed two chopsticks between my father's fingers. "Hold the bottom chopstick still. Move the top one to pick up the food," the waiter said.

My father tried, but the meat slipped off his chopstick and fell on his lap.

The waiter came back with a bowl of soup. How can I eat soup with chopsticks? my father thought.

"Drink," said the waiter. "Drink from the bowl."

"Thank goodness," my father said. After the soup my father felt better. He picked up the chopsticks. Finally, my father put one piece of meat in his mouth. Delicious!

"More soup, please," he said.

After three bowls of soup my father felt much better. Then he practiced some more with his chopsticks. Soon, there was more sukiyaki in his belly than on the floor. But it was too late to call my mother. He had to run back to his ship.

That night, my mother was sad. Every other day my father had come to see her. That day he did not come. He did not call on the telephone. Perhaps he was tired of walking and talking. Perhaps he was ashamed of her because she did not know how to eat with a knife and fork. Perhaps his ship had sailed away. All night she could not sleep.

And all night my father sat on his bunk, pretending to pick up sukiyaki.

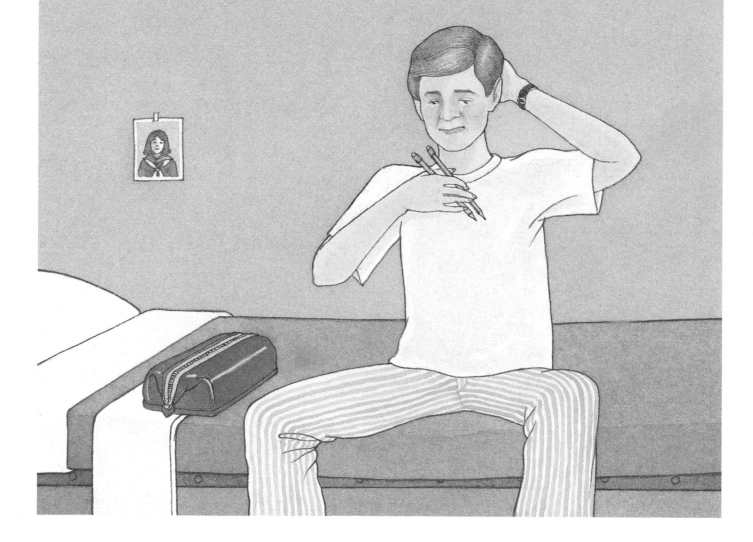

The next morning my father called my mother. "Please, will you eat dinner with me tonight?"

"Yes!" my mother shouted into the phone. First she was happy. Then she was afraid. She took her schoolbooks and ran to the house of Great Uncle.

Great Uncle had visited England. He had seen the British Museum. He had eaten dinners with Englishmen.

My mother knocked at the door. Great Uncle opened it.

"Why are you so sad, child?" he asked.

"Because I must learn to eat with a knife and fork by seven o'clock tonight."

Great Uncle nodded. "Foreign ways are quite strange. Why do you want to eat with a knife and fork?"

My mother blushed.

"Is it the American sailor?" Great Uncle asked. "I see . . . Here, take this note to your teacher. At lunchtime I will come and take you to a foreign restaurant. By seven o'clock tonight you will eat with a knife and fork."

My mother picked up her school bag and bowed.

"No," Great Uncle stuck out his hand. "In the West you shake hands."

The restaurant had red carpets and many lights. Great Uncle pulled out a chair for my mother. "In the West, men help ladies into chairs," he told her.

My mother looked at the small fork and the large fork on the left. She looked at the knife, little spoon, and big spoon on the right. Her head grew dizzy.

"Different utensils for different foods," Great Uncle said.

"How strange to dirty so many things," said my mother. "A chopstick is a chopstick. I can eat everything with two chopsticks."

When the waiter brought the soup, Great Uncle pointed at the large spoon. "Dip it slowly, bring it to your mouth. Sip quietly."

My mother's hand trembled. The soup spilled onto the white cloth.

"You'll learn," Great Uncle encouraged her.

When my mother was finished with the soup, the waiter brought her a plate of mashed potatoes, roast beef, and peas.

"This is the way Westerners eat," Great Uncle said. "With the knife and fork they cut the meat. Then they hold the fork upside down in their left hand. Like birds, they build a nest of mashed potatoes. They put the peas in the nest with the knife. Then they slip the nest into their mouth. Try it."

The mashed potatoes were not difficult. But the peas rolled all over the plate. "Impossible," said my mother. "I'll never learn by seven o'clock tonight."

"You can learn anything," Great Uncle said. "Try again. More mashed potatoes and peas, please," he said to the waiter.

At seven o'clock my father came to see my mother.

"Why didn't you wear your kimono?" he asked. "We are going to a Japanese restaurant."

"A Japanese restaurant? Don't you think I know how to eat Western food?" my mother asked.

"Of course. Don't you think I know how to eat Japanese food?"

"Of course."

"Then, tonight we'll eat meat and potatoes. Tomorrow night we'll eat sukiyaki."

"Tomorrow night I will wear my kimono," my mother said. She started to bow. Then she stopped and put out her hand. My father shook it.

My father ordered two plates of mashed potatoes, roast beef, and peas. He watched my mother cut the meat into pieces. He stared when she turned over her fork and made a bird's nest. He was amazed.

"You are very clever with a knife and fork," he said.

"Thank you," said my mother.

"You must teach me," my father said. "That's a new way of eating peas."

"Teach you?"

"Yes, Americans don't eat that way." He slid his fork under some peas and put them in his mouth.

My mother stared at him. "But Great Uncle taught me. He lived in England. He knows the ways of the West."

My father began to laugh. "He taught you to eat like an Englishman. Americans eat differently."

"Oh, dear," my mother said. "A chopstick is a chopstick. Everyone uses them in the same way."

"Yes. When we are married we'll eat only with chopsticks." He took her hand.

"Married! If I marry you I want to eat like an American."

"I'll teach you to eat with a knife and fork and you teach me to use chopsticks."

My mother shook my father's hand. My father bowed.

That's why at our house some days we eat with chopsticks and some days we eat with knives and forks.